Big Sky Mountain

Big Sky Mountain

ALEX MILWAY

Piccadilly
PRESS

First published in Great Britain in 2021 by
PICCADILLY PRESS
80-81 Wimpole Street, London W1G 9RE
Owned by Bonnier Books
Sveavägen 56, Stockholm, Sweden
www.piccadillypress.co.uk

A CIP catalogue record for this book is available from the British Library.
ISBN: 978-1-84812-972-6
Also available as an ebook and audio
1

Printed and bound in China

Piccadilly Press is an imprint of Bonnier Books UK
www.bonnierbooks.co.uk

For Gran, tough as old boots
and absolutely fearless

1
Grandma Nan

After an hour of travelling across miles of wilderness, the tiny plane carrying Rosa Wild dipped down and landed effortlessly on Jewel Lake. It chugged slowly across the water, its twin floats sending ripples across the glassy surface.

'Here we are then,' said Tom, the pilot. 'Quite something, huh? Told you this place was unlike anywhere on earth.'

Rosa sat up in the back seat and gazed in wonder – and no small amount of panic – at the boulder-strewn slopes and spire-like trees that rose up around her. The emptiness of Big Sky Mountain and the never-ending horizon was terrifying to someone who'd only ever known the city.

'It's so . . . big!' said Rosa.

Tom's moustache twitched as he cut power to the engines and sailed the plane towards the gravelly beach.

'It definitely is that,' said Tom.

'And where are all the houses and shops?' asked Rosa.

Tom laughed. 'About two hundred

miles away,' he said. He pointed through the window. 'There's your grandma now. She always hears me coming in to land.'

Rosa pulled her heavy cloth bag tight to her chest. She had never met Grandma Nan before, and seeing the wild-haired old lady striding out of the trees towards them, Rosa feared the worst. She didn't look like the sort who appreciated visitors.

'Will you come back?' asked Rosa hopefully.

'Next delivery's in a few months,' said Tom.

'That long?' said Rosa.

'Uh-huh,' he replied, getting out of the pilot's seat. He pushed open the door and hung his legs out as the plane gradually stopped moving. A burst of fresh air entered the cockpit. 'Nan looks after herself, but she always likes her winter supplies brought in early before the lake freezes over.'

'It freezes over?' said Rosa.

'Oh, sure,' said Tom, dropping out on to one of the long floats that took the place of landing wheels. 'Come on.'

Rosa clambered over boxes filled with

tins of fruit and powdered milk, and all the sorts of dried food that might last a year or two in a cupboard. She stepped down, and Tom helped her cross the float on to dry land.

Grandma Nan stood watching with a puzzled air.

'Who's this then?' she asked. She wiped her thick glasses, hoping cleaner lenses might change her view. 'I didn't ask you to bring me a girl, Tom.'

'It's Rosa,' said Rosa. 'Your granddaughter.'

Nan smeared down her bristly shock of hair – it promptly leapt back into place – and walked closer.

'Granddaughter, eh?' said Nan. 'Rosa?'

'I sent you a letter about coming to stay,' said Rosa.

'She did,' said Tom. 'I delivered it myself.'

Nan scrunched up her nose in thought.

'I don't remember reading a letter,' she said. 'But I do have a granddaughter –'

'While you discuss this,' said Tom with

a smile, 'I best get all your supplies out and move on. There's a storm rolling in from the north.'

'I heard the crows warning of it this morning,' said Grandma Nan.

'Course you did, Nan,' said Tom.

Nan peered down at Rosa. 'Are you sure you're my granddaughter?' she said, her eyes peeking over the top of her glasses. 'She's just a baby.'

Rosa caught sight of a naughty twinkle in her eyes. Was she playing a game?

'We have the same name,' said Rosa. 'You're a Wild. I'm a Wild.'

'You don't look very wild.'

Grandma Nan squeezed Rosa's arm in search of muscles. Her grip was as strong as a vice.

'And you don't *feel* too wild either,' said Nan. 'You're all skin and bone.'

Rosa pulled her arm free. 'Look. I am a Wild,' said Rosa, 'and –'

'And what?' said Nan.

Rosa was edging close to tears. 'And I don't have anywhere else to go,' she said.

Grandma Nan huffed. 'It's true. A girl's got to be in a real pickle to end up out here,' said Nan.

Tom placed the last box of supplies on the gravel.

'Right, that's it then!' he said. 'You'll be OK, Rosa?'

Rosa wasn't sure. 'What happens if we need help?' she asked.

'We won't need help,' said Nan with a shake of the head. 'I've lived out here for twenty-three years so far, and look at me! Still alive.'

'Told you,' said Tom. 'Nan looks after herself better than anyone. She'll see you right.'

And with a smile and a salute Tom was back in the plane. The engine kicked into life and within seconds he was motoring along the water, building up speed for take-off.

The plane rose into the air and disappeared over the mountain.

The world was silent once more.

'Well, this is something,' said Nan, thrusting her hands on to her hips.

Rosa slung her bag over her shoulder. 'I *am* your granddaughter,' said Rosa.

'I know you are,' said Nan. 'You have my eyebrows.'

She picked up a crate of tins and marched off into the trees. 'This way! And bring a box!'

Rosa grabbed a box of dried beans and hurried on. Birds were chattering in the trees, butterflies were whispering, and even the midges buzzing about her head seemed to have things to say. If Rosa hadn't known better, she'd have thought they were all discussing her arrival. Little did she know there was a big surprise in store for her.

The Cabin

Grandma Nan's log cabin was like
something from an old fairy tale, nestled
at the edge of the lake among a glade of
towering pine trees. Built solely of wood,
with a tatty pitched roof covered in a
layer of moss and earth, the cabin was full
of imperfections. Knotholes littered the
walls, cracks between planks and beams
were filled with glue and thread, and the

tilting stone chimney had so many weeds growing out of the mortar that it could have been mistaken for having hair.

'Home sweet home,' said Grandma Nan.

Rosa looked on in horror. 'I thought you lived in a house?' she said. 'This place looks like it could fall apart at any minute!'

Nan kicked the wall beside the door. There was a loud thud, but nothing broke, fell off or budged an inch.

'It would take a battering ram to move it, my girl,' said Nan. 'I should know. I did build it, after all.'

Rosa gulped. 'Don't builders usually build homes?'

'You try finding a builder out here,'

said Nan, pulling open the door. 'Come on in. And don't mind Albert; he won't bite.'

'Wait!' said Rosa. 'I thought you lived alone?'

'I do,' said Nan. 'More or less.'

Rosa stepped inside and inhaled the rich, tarry smell of seasoned wood. Despite her first impressions, it was homely and warm, and though it was really just one giant room, it felt like so much more.

There was a tidy bed covered in a brightly coloured crocheted blanket. Next to it was a stone fireplace, with a nest of logs prepared ready for lighting. There was a potbelly iron stove, bearing a blackened pan and kettle, and every wooden wall was decorated with handmade rugs and cupboards.

And then Rosa froze. A moose head – with huge antlers – was sticking through an open window at the back of the cabin. It turned to look at her with happy yet tired eyes.

'Mornin',' said the moose in a low grumbly voice. 'I never seen a hooman calf before.'

Rosa looked wide-eyed at Grandma Nan who was zipping back and forth across the small room, packing tins away in storage and on to shelves.

'Meet Albert,' said Nan.

'Is he dangerous?' asked Rosa.

'Only to himself,' said Nan. 'Albert gets

into trouble easier than finding pebbles on the beach.'

'Hey!' huffed Albert. 'I got ears.'

Grandma Nan had a deep throaty laugh and she chuckled loudly. Rosa crept forward, rightly unsure of the giant animal. She'd never been as close to any creature so big before.

'Hello . . . sir?' said Rosa nervously.

Albert's giant head stretched forward through the window and sniffed Rosa's forehead. 'Hooman calf smells of pink flowers,' he said.

'Thank you,' said Rosa.

'Don't worry, she'll soon smell of rotten potatoes like the rest of us,' said Nan, passing Rosa an apple. 'Here, I bet he's hungry.'

'Apple!' pleaded Albert, and before Rosa had a chance to offer it, the moose's slobbery teeth had clamped on to the fruit.

He tried to retreat back out of the window to eat, but his antlers were too wide. They bumped against the wooden frame on each side.

'Head stuck,' growled Albert.

DONK!

Nan rolled her eyes. 'Every year when his antlers grow back it's like this . . .' She hurried over and took hold of Albert's left antler. 'I wish I knew how you got them in so easily.'

With a bit of a twist Nan found a better angle for Albert's head.

'Try it now,' she said, and he finally pulled free.

'Stupid head,' said Albert, and he wandered off to the beach to eat.

'He spends every summer here,' said Nan. 'I never know where he goes after, but he always returns to the mountain each and every year.'

Rosa wondered what it must be like to be the only human for a hundred miles around.

'Don't you get lonely out here?' asked Rosa.

'Lonely is the last thing I am,' said Nan. 'I came here to get away from the world, but can barely go a minute without seeing someone.'

'Where?' said Rosa. She peered out through the window at the surrounding wilderness. There were no other houses to be seen.

'Everywhere,' said Nan. 'Albert's one.'

'But he's a moose?' said Rosa.

'There's not much difference between them and us,' said Nan, returning to her unpacking and tidying.

Nan was overjoyed by the new deliveries, and read every label on every tin as though it were an exciting new book.

'Can I help?' asked Rosa.

'You could unpack your things,' said Nan. 'Key to living in here is to keep everything tidy. You are tidy, aren't you?'

'Yes,' squeaked Rosa awkwardly and not fully truthfully. 'Where should I put them?'

Nan pointed to a cupboard.

'And where will I be sleeping?' said Rosa.

'Well, I've only got one bed,' said Nan, 'so I guess we'll be sharing.'

'Together?' said Rosa.

Nan shrugged. 'You don't snore do you? I hate snorers.'

'No, of course

I don't,' said Rosa, though she wondered how anyone could know. 'But it's such a tiny bed.'

'There's always the floor,' said Nan matter-of-factly.

Rosa looked at the hard, cold floorboards.

'Sharing it is,' she said.

3

New Arrivals

Just as Tom had warned, the storm came good and strong. Rosa and Nan enjoyed watching the violent weather from the comfort of the cabin. As the trees roared about them, with the scouring growl of pouring rain the surface of the lake was pocked with thousands of craters. But there was not one leak or drip of water falling from the ceiling, much to Rosa's surprise.

'Is Albert all right out there?' asked Rosa.

'That moose could survive a hurricane,' said Nan. 'He'll be hiding somewhere, I'm sure. But don't worry, storms pass quickly out here.'

Slowly but surely the clouds broke apart, and sunlight burst through.

'I love a storm,' said Nan, preparing to head outside. 'It shakes the world up. Brings out all sorts of creatures.'

With her boots pulled high Nan strode out into the world.

'What are you waiting for?' she said, heading off down to the lake.

Rosa readied herself and walked out under the eaves of the roof. A thin cord of water dripped from its edge, and Rosa played with it for a moment, passing her hands through each drip trying to not get wet. Suddenly she heard a hoot of a yawn from above her head.

Rosa looked up, just in time, to see a tiny owl roll out of a crevice in the cabin wall. It tumbled out, still half asleep, and Rosa caught it safely in her hands.

The owl's eyes blinked and opened wide.

'Hello, little bird,' said Rosa.

'SAVE ME!'

screeched the owl, covering its face with its small wings. 'SAVE ME!'

'From what?!' asked Rosa calmly. She could feel its heart beating fast through her fingers.

The owl peeked out through a gap in its feathers. It turned its head nearly full circle, before looking up at Rosa.

'Oh . . . is it over?' it said tentatively, before ruffling its feathers and stretching out its legs. 'Nothing to see here. This owl is fine! Move along please!'

'Were you having a nightmare?' said Rosa.

The owl blinked with amazing slowness.

'Might have been,' said the owl sniffily. 'Might not have been.'

28

'Well, I'm just pleased I caught you,' said Rosa. 'It was a long drop for a little thing like you.'

'Who are you calling little?' said the owl.

Rosa lifted the owl to eye height so she could see it more closely. The owl really was tiny – hardly bigger than Rosa's hand.

'You are very cute,' said Rosa.

'That's the rudest thing anyone has ever said to me,' said the owl. 'Now put me back, please.'

The owl frowned and crossed its wings in an attempt to look strong and fearsome, but Rosa thought it simply made the bird look even cuter. She smiled and placed the bird back in its crevice.

'There you go,' said Rosa.

The owl skipped from her hand to hide once again in the cabin wall.

'You can go away now,' it said. 'Go on. Shoo!'

Rosa laughed and walked off towards Grandma Nan.

'I've just met your owl!' said Rosa.

'Oh no. That's not *my* owl,' said Nan. 'And you best not let him hear you say that. Little Pig is very much his own owl.'

'He's called Little Pig?' said Rosa.

'That's right,' said Nan. 'He's a pygmy owl, and a particularly small one. Little Pig suits him very well.'

Nan turned her head to the north and cupped her ears. 'Hang about – you hear that noise?' she said.

Rosa listened intently. With the storm off to bother another mountain, the birds were chattering again, but beyond that noise was a grumbling growl, growing closer by the second.

'Thunder again?' asked Rosa.

Grandma Nan dug her hands into her deep trouser pockets – the sort of pockets

that you can bury a full sandwich in –
and pulled out a collapsing telescope. She
stretched it open and aimed it at the sky.

The silhouette of a large plane
eventually appeared from beyond the
mountain peak. It coursed across the sky,
leaving spiralling vapour trails in its wake.

'Now who on earth could that be?'
said Nan. 'It's not Tom.'

A speck of light glinted off the aircraft and two parachutes bloomed from its hold and took flight.

'Well, blow my trumpet loud and long,' said Nan. 'Here –'

She thrust the telescope into Rosa's hand.

'Look at that!' said Nan.

Rosa held the telescope to her eye and spent a frantic moment searching for the parachutes through the narrow lens. She gasped when she found them, and saw that they were attached to two brown furry creatures. They drifted down over a distant tree-covered hill.

'What are they?' asked Rosa.

'Too far away for me to be sure,' said Grandma Nan, 'though they look like trouble. We'll need to investigate.'

'But they must have landed miles away!' said Rosa.

'Three, maybe four,' said Nan. 'A good day's hike.'

'That's a long way,' said Rosa.

'It is,' said Nan.

'But you're –'

'Go on, say it,' said Nan.

Rosa suddenly felt awful. 'I . . . Well . . . well, you are a bit old.'

'And I hope your legs are stronger than your mind,' said Nan. 'So pull yourself together, girl. I've lived out here a long time now, and I know what I'm capable of.'

'Sorry,' said Rosa. 'It's just that you're not really like other grandmas. They just sit and watch TV. Or snooze. Or bake cakes. Or –'

Grandma Nan lifted her glasses to rub her eyes.

'I like to think that's no bad thing, is it?' she said warmly.

'I suppose not,' said Rosa.

Nan strode off towards the cabin.

'RIGHT! Come on! We best pack some supplies. We can't carry too much, but *Florence* can take the worst of it.'

'Who's Florence?' asked Rosa.

'You'll see,' said Nan, taking a deep breath of mountain air. 'And I best warn you about the early start.'

'How early?' said Rosa.

'The sun rises at five in the morning,' said Nan. 'We need to make the most of the daylight – there are no street lamps where we're going!'

Rosa was quick to realise that life on Big Sky Mountain was going to be very different to what she was used to.

Florence

It was an uncomfortable night. Rosa quickly got over sharing a bed with her grandma, but because of her very loud snoring she couldn't sleep – and the eerie howls of wolves somewhere outside kept her eyes locked open and sent shivers down her spine.

Twice she got up to check that the incredibly thick cabin door was locked, just to be sure, and twice she found it was. Yet at no point in all of Rosa's shuffling about in the dark and bumping into chairs and tables did Grandma Nan wake up.

Only the occasional hoot and screech – which Rosa thought must belong to Little Pig – made her feel more comfortable. If that tiny owl could survive out in the wilderness, with wolves running wild, so could she.

When the sun's golden glow finally pierced the windowpane and cut a beam through the cabin, Rosa felt even more tired than she had before going to bed. She scraped away the sleep from her eyes as Grandma Nan rolled over and sat up on the edge of the bed, her feet falling precisely into her shoes. Nan's fingers then dropped down exactly on the spot where she'd stored her glasses the previous night, and she slotted them on to her nose.

'Looks like a day for an adventure,' she said, stretching her arms out wide. She rubbed Rosa firmly on the shoulder. 'Rise and shine, my girl, we have a mountain to climb!'

After a breakfast of pancakes and freshly picked berries, they headed out towards the lake. The morning was crisp and fresh, and after yesterday's storm the air was beautifully rich with smells.

'Here she is!' said Nan, throwing her backpack into a long red canoe.

'Who?' said Rosa.

'*Florence*,' said Nan. 'My trusty old canoe. Here, grab hold –'

Grandma Nan passed Rosa the oar, who looked at it as though it was the most ridiculous item she'd ever seen.

'And you want me to row?' said Rosa.

'I'm going to make a mountain girl out of you, that's for sure,' said Nan.

'But I don't know how to row,' said Rosa.

'Oh, in you get!' said Nan. 'Just because you've never done something, doesn't mean you won't be any good at it.'

Rosa looked uncertain.

'Will everything be all right here, though?' she asked. 'I could stay to keep watch?'

'Don't be ridiculous, girl. I've got my own burglar alarm,' said Nan.

Nan called back to the cabin. 'Keep watch, Little Pig!'

The owl hooted a reply and Nan slid the red canoe into the water. She held it while Rosa clambered in, then pushed it gently and threw herself inside. The canoe bobbed and dipped, eventually righting itself on the lake.

A spray of ice-cold water hit Rosa in the face.

'It's freezing,' spluttered Rosa.

'Don't I know it,' said Nan. 'If we tip over out here, chances are the water will finish you off before you reach shore.'

'It's that cold?' asked Rosa fearfully.

'It is. Respect the water and you won't get hurt,' said Nan. 'Now, come on, we've got some critters to find.'

Rosa dipped the paddle into the water and pulled. 'Like this?' she said.

Nan nodded, but the canoe barely moved forward. It turned a slow circle.

'We'll never get anywhere at this rate,' said Nan.

'I'm trying!' said Rosa.

She pushed the paddle through the water again, but the canoe only turned faster.

The water started to bubble around them, and three fish heads popped up into the air. The surprise made Rosa drop the paddle, which slowly drifted away.

'That's a relief!' said a trout, attempting to nudge the paddle further out into the lake.

'You're telling me!' cheered the second fish.

'All that spinning was making me dizzy!' said the third fish.

'All right, that's enough complaining,' said Grandma Nan to the fish, rolling her eyes. 'Rosa, meet the Fins: April, May and June.'

Rosa snatched the end of the paddle before the fish could move it out of reach and pulled it into the boat.

'How do you do, Rosie?' said April.

'She's not Rosie, she's Roly,' said May.

'No, no, no,' said June. 'She's not Roly, she's Nosy.'

Grandma Nan shook her head.

'They always have an opinion on something or other,' she said. 'You'll get used to them – in a few years.'

Rosa leant over the side of the canoe to see them better.

'It's Rosa,' she said.

'Told you!' said April, turning to the others. It raised its fin in greeting. 'Pleased to meet you!'

'Are we?' said May.

'I'm not so sure,' said June. 'Her paddling is awful.'

'She will get better,' said Nan. 'Now could you please let us continue on our journey? Rosa needs practice.'

'You only had to ask,' said April.

'Imagine if we were as bad at swimming!' said May.

'Doesn't bear thinking about,' said June.

And with that they all flopped back under the water. A final few bubbles popped at the surface, and they were gone.

'Like I said,' said Grandma Nan, 'whether you like it or not, you're never alone out here.'

Rosa pulled at the water once more with the paddle, and gradually, under Nan's guidance, she got the hang of it.

'We're going forward!' cheered Rosa.

'Keep it up!' said Nan, smiling.

The canoe cut a gentle course across the lake, and Rosa filled with excitement. There was nothing ahead of her but the wilderness: open water, mountains, valleys, trees and a huge shimmering sky. So this was what it felt like to be a wild animal, thought Rosa – to be free. It was a new feeling for her, and it was wonderful.

5

Down Gold River

The lake was long and they took it in
turns to paddle for what seemed like
hours to Rosa. Only the sun's slow creep
into the sky and the occasional bird
swooping over the lake gave her any sense
of time passing.

Rosa wasn't used to silence – the city
was always noisy – so she tried to find
ways of filling the gap. She hummed

happy songs. Nan didn't like that. She whistled tuneless tunes. Nan liked that even less. In the end she settled for asking questions to pass the time. Foremost on her mind were the wolves she'd heard in the night.

'Grandma Nan,' said Rosa, 'do you get many wolves around here?'

'Lots,' said Nan. 'I've never had the pleasure of chatting to one, but from what I've been told they're a surly bunch. Like to keep themselves to themselves.'

'It's just that I heard lots of them out on the mountain last night,' said Rosa.

'I take it you didn't sleep well then?' asked Nan.

'No, not really,' said Rosa. 'Are they dangerous? The wolves?'

'Definitely,' said Nan. 'But then, so are humans.'

That didn't ease Rosa's mind at all.

As slow going as it was, they made good progress along the lake. The hills drew closer together and formed a solid barrier ahead, but for a narrow river cutting straight through.

'Here we are,' said Nan. 'Gold River. It'll lead us out all the way to the waterfall.'

'That sounds dangerous,' said Rosa.

'We're not going down it,' said Nan. 'But you best pass me the paddle.'

Rosa did as she was told and settled in for the ride.

The canoe zigzagged through the narrow channels in between rocks.

Grandma Nan was an old hand at this, and though Rosa gripped on for dear life, she knew she was in safe hands.

'Once passed this section, it's plain sailing,' said Nan, enjoying the challenge. 'But we're heading into Angry Territory, so stay alert.'

'Angry Territory?' asked Rosa.

'That's right,' said Nan. She flicked the paddle firmly, steering past a large mossy boulder. Water splashed up into the canoe, soaking Rosa's shoes. 'Mr Pernicky lives near here. He has moods and he has them good.'

'Who's Mr Pernicky?' asked Rosa.

'A mountain hare,' said Nan. 'And the grumpiest old boot on Big Sky Mountain.'

They travelled on for another few minutes as the river's flow grew stronger and the canoe sailed faster.

'Almost there,' said Nan. 'Get ready!'

'Ready for what?' said Rosa.

'Lunch,' said Nan.

The hills gradually sank away, the river widened and Nan steered the canoe across to the river's edge before it became too difficult to control. Not too far away, the roaring river vanished from view and thundered down as a waterfall.

'This'll do,' said Nan, before driving them up on to a gravelly beach. She leapt out and held the boat steady for Rosa. 'Nothing like paddling a canoe to build up an appetite. Hungry?'

'Never been hungrier,' said Rosa.

But food was delayed. They heard a scuffling, shuffling noise behind them among a stand of trees and thick prickly bushes.

'What's that?' said Rosa, fearful.

Nan grabbed the oar for protection.

RUSTLE

'Who is it?' she called.

But there was no reply. The bushes
bustled and crunched, and finally their
branches were pushed apart by a pair of
giant paws with very long claws.

6

The Travelling Sales Bear

A lolloping bear tumbled out into the open, only to spend the next few seconds unhooking his long blue scarf from a cluster of thorns.

'Give it back,' he muttered to the bush, tugging it firmly.

Rosa squeaked a scream and readied to run, but she had nothing to fear. This was no ordinary bear, made clear by

the fact that he was carrying a heavy backpack.

'Did someone mention food?' said the bear, finally freeing his scarf.

Grandma Nan dropped her guard and smiled.

'It's only my old friend Mr Hibberdee,' she said happily. 'You shouldn't go creeping about out here. What are you up to?'

The bear shrugged and scratched his plentiful stomach. 'I'm just out following the clouds,' he said. 'And selling my goods, of course.'

He loosened his backpack to the ground and opened the largest pocket.

'What do you fancy? I've got jams of all sorts, from berry to plum, some

extra special marshmallows and –'
Mr Hibberdee smacked his lips – 'my
bestselling heather honey. Ready to do
a good deal for you, Nan!'

'You're too kind, Mr Hibberdee,' said
Nan. 'Anything take your fancy, Rosa?'

'I . . . I'm not sure,' said Rosa, still
very wary of the giant bear.

'Oh, don't worry about him,' said Nan. 'He's gentle as anything.'

Mr Hibberdee plodded closer to Rosa and patted her on the head. His strength almost drilled her into the ground.

'She has a nice head for patting,' said the bear. 'Also, as she's a new customer, I best give you a taster. How does that sound?'

'I wouldn't pass up an opportunity like that,' said Nan.

'What do you like best?' said Mr Hibberdee. 'Jam or honey?'

Rosa had to think hard on this. 'Umm . . .' she said, looking to Nan for guidance. 'Probably honey.'

'Heather honey it is!' said the bear.

He pulled out a packet of crackers

from his backpack and twisted the lid on a jar of honey. As soon as the sweet aroma hit his nose, his eyes started to glow. He looked a bit dizzy.

'Are you all right?' asked Rosa.

'It's the honey, that's all,' said Mr Hibberdee. 'It goes right to my brain. Honest, you won't find a better pot of honey in all the world. Comes straight from the bees on Prickly Plain.'

He dipped a cracker into the thick golden syrup and passed it to Rosa. She took a bite. It was rich and sweet and tasted of a long, warm summer.

'YUM!' said Rosa. 'It's delicious.'

Mr Hibberdee dipped in another cracker and threw it into his mouth.

'One for my customer, one for me,' he

said to Nan, chewing and gulping.

'So,' said Mr Hibberdee, licking a few drops of spilt honey from his paw, 'you want to buy a jar?'

Rosa looked awkwardly at her grandma. 'I don't have any money,' she whispered.

'You don't need money,' said Nan.

'But how do I pay?' asked Rosa.

'We trade in everything around here,' said the bear. 'Time, stories, food. If the proposition is good, the deal's on!'

Rosa was a little bit lost for words. She didn't really have anything to trade.

'I tell you what,' said Mr Hibberdee kindly. 'Since you're new, and you look trustworthy, have a think and pay me later. Is that a deal?'

'If you don't mind,' said Rosa.

'Not at all,' said Mr Hibberdee. 'I shall come and find you. I never forget a sale!'

He took out a full jar of honey and handed it over to Rosa.

'And I best be making a move then,' he said. 'Places to go. Goods to sell!'

'Watch out for those brambles,' said Nan.

Mr Hibberdee shook his fist.

'Grrrrr!' he said, and wandered off into the forest, whistling happily. Rosa looked happily at the jar of honey.

'You've done well there,' said Nan.

'I just hope I can pay him for it,' said Rosa.

'There's nothing a bear likes more than a good story,' said Nan. 'You must have a few of those?'

Rosa thought hard about it for a few moments, but struggled to come up with anything.

'I don't think I do,' she said.

Grandma Nan pulled the canoe further on to dry land and tied it to a tree.

'Perhaps something will come to you on our walk?' she said. 'I get my best ideas wandering the mountain.'

Nan and Rosa trekked along the river, eventually reaching the wide, surging waterfall. There was a mountain goats' path wending its way down through boulders and grassy outcrops, and Nan ushered Rosa safely along the dangerous route.

A thick cloud of sparkling mist billowed skywards, cloaking Rosa and Nan in a damp fog. When they reached the bottom Rosa looked up at the glistening sheet of rippling water that fell at least fifty metres to the crystal-clear pool at its base.

'Dilly-dally Falls,' said Nan. 'Nowhere quite as beautiful as this to eat your lunch.'

Rosa could only agree. They spent the next hour sharing bread, honey and Grandma Nan's homemade raspberry biscuits at the base of the waterfall. The frothing roar of the water was enough to make Rosa feel sleepy, and before long her eyes were feeling heavy.

Grandma Nan sat happily with her

feet in the pool, while Rosa fell asleep, lulled into a dream by the frothing roar of the water.

7

The Angry Mountain Hare

Rosa could have slept for days, but Grandma Nan was always one to keep moving.

'That'll do, or else we'll never make it before dark,' said Nan, gently squeezing Rosa's shoulder.

They collected their things and set off into the lush forest, following the river. Tree trunks blocked any view of what lay ahead: some were thin and white, while some were giants that would take thirty people holding hands to wrap fully round their base.

But then, as they walked further into

the wilderness, they came upon something very strange. The trees grew thin, until suddenly there were none. Where once there were towering trees, now sat gnawed stumps and a thick carpet of wood chippings. And right in the middle of it all, bouncing around like a rabid pogo stick, was a furious mountain hare.

'Look at this mess!' cried Mr Pernicky. 'My great-grandparents hopped through here, arm in arm, and now it's all –'

Mr Pernicky's ears wobbled and fizzed, eventually shooting bolt upright.

'GONE!' he screamed.

The hare bounded about the forest floor in a rage, his ears rocketing up and down as he rose and fell.

'Take it easy, Mr Pernicky,' said Grandma Nan. 'There is likely to be a perfectly reasonable explanation.'

'Reasonable?!' he said. He bounced forward and pushed his little button nose into Nan's face. 'There is nothing reasonable about these creatures! They have slimy, oily fur, and don't get me started on their orange teeth!

They are disgusting!!!'

'MR PERNICKY!' pleaded Grandma Nan. 'Please, calm down.'

But Mr Pernicky found it impossible to calm down. He was a hare and he was in a mad rage!

'They come over here, drop out of the skies and claim the land for their own!' he said.

Rosa watched the hare's face redden and redden until he reached boiling point.

'Enough!' said Grandma Nan.

The hare was set to explode.

He twisted his bow tie and let it spin back into place.

'Who are they?' asked Rosa.

'Vile, horrible creatures!' said Mr Pernicky.

'I very much doubt that,' said Nan.

'You wait till you meet them!' said the hare. 'They won't listen.'

Mr Pernicky led the way along the river, which was running fuller than usual.

'There they are!' he said angrily. 'Look at them. Eating more trees!'

'Aha!' said Grandma Nan, smiling. 'That's what came out of the plane. Beavers!'

Two brown-furred beavers were hard at work on the riverside, chewing at tree bark from fallen trunks. Their orange

teeth were so
bright they
almost glowed.

'Are they
dangerous?'
asked Rosa.

'They'll chew
your ears off if you take your eyes off
them for even one second!' said Mr
Pernicky.

'Oh, stop it. They absolutely wouldn't
hurt a fly,' said Nan.

One of the beavers suddenly realised
they were being watched. She slammed
her tail against the ground and dived into
the water. The other didn't seem quite
so bothered. She stopped chewing and
peered out across the river.

'Who's that then?' she said with a wave of her paw.

Grandma Nan marched over to the riverside. 'Afternoon!' she said. 'You're new here?'

'That's right,' said the creature. 'Elsie Beaver. And that one's Iris.'

'So, what brings you to Big Sky Mountain?' asked Nan.

Elsie pulled out a document from within her fur and held it aloft.

'We've been relocated,' she said.

'Fascinating,' said Nan. 'What for?'

'Official rewilding purposes,' said Elsie. 'This here paper is the document saying exactly so.'

'I see,' said Nan.

Rosa looked at the sheet

of paper, which consisted of a map and some building plans. Whatever the beavers were up to looked incredibly grand, she thought.

'You didn't waste any time getting started,' said Rosa.

The beaver revealed that the piece of wood she was chewing was actually a big signpost saying BEAVER TOWN. She'd dug out the letters with her teeth.

'Because there's so much to get done!' said Elsie. She skipped about the riverbank pointing at things that weren't there.

'Where are the reeds? The willows? The dragonflies?'

'I don't know,' said Rosa.

'Exactly!' she said. 'They should be in the shallows at the water's edge, but there aren't any shallows because of these steep riverbanks.'

Elsie stretched down and dipped her paw into the river. She held it there for effect, as the water drove forcefully against it.

'You know why they're so steep?' she asked.

Rosa shrugged.

'Because the water runs too fast,' said Elsie. 'And when it runs too fast, the river cuts deeper, down and down into the earth, and the riverbanks grow up and up.'

'I see,' said Rosa. 'But why's that a problem?'

'Oh, don't get me started!' said Elsie. 'Where are the young fish and baby waterbirds supposed to grow up?!'

'I don't know,' said Rosa.

'I can tell you they won't survive a minute in there. They'll be flushed out to sea,' said Elsie.

'That's awful,' said Rosa.

'And that's not mentioning all the flooding after winter or storms. The river swells, grows even faster and destroys everything in its path – until it dumps all its water on the lowlands. Such a waste, when we need it here.'

'We do?' said Rosa.

'Absolutely,' said Elsie. 'We need to

slow down the water and free it from the river. If we spread it out, it can feed all this forest. Plants will soon come back, I promise. As will the baby fish!'

'I didn't know how important your jobs were,' said Rosa.

'No one does,' said Elsie. 'So you can see we have our work cut out.'

By now Mr Pernicky was almost turning purple. 'You make me want to scream!' he said. 'This river is perfect. And this is not Beaver Town. This is Pernicky Town!'

The river water darkened, and Iris, the second beaver, popped her head out of the water, raising an armful of thin branches.

'Afternoon,' said Iris, before vanishing again underwater.

'And what's she doing down there?' asked Mr Pernicky.

'Building,' said Elsie.

Mr Pernicky's eyes started to spin. 'I need a sit down,' he said, before promptly fainting.

Rosa hurried to him and held him on his side while he came round. His eyes blinked slowly.

'Beavers . . .' he muttered in a daze. 'Everywhere . . .'

'I think we ought to get him home,' said Rosa.

'I think you're right,' said Grandma Nan.

8

This . . . Is . . . War!

Rosa and Grandma Nan took one paw each and helped Mr Pernicky to his home at the riverside. The hare lived in a wooden shack, although to describe it as such was a great disservice: at least three times taller than Grandma Nan's cabin, his home dominated the forest like a wooden mansion within landscaped grounds. Two perfectly square towers sprouted from its walls, and a windmill stood tall on the roof, spinning gently in the breeze above the tree canopy.

Mr Pernicky was evidently a master craftsman, excellent with joints and joists, who also loved to grow things and tend his garden. There were little boxes under the cabin's windows, all stuffed with brightly coloured plants and heather, and surrounding it were very well-kept vegetable patches full of carrots.

The smell of his home helped Mr Pernicky feel more normal. He unlatched the door and they went inside. It was a small opening for such a grand place, but Rosa could just about fit inside without ducking. Nan stooped low, stepped in and closed the door behind her.

Grandma Nan knew Mr Pernicky had recovered fully when he started grumping again.

'Those creatures have no right to be here,' he grumbled. 'This . . . is . . . war.'

'Doesn't everyone have a right to live here?' said Rosa. 'I thought this place belonged to everyone?'

'But there is the whole mountain!' he said. 'There are hundreds and hundreds of miles of nothingness out there. Why do they need to live on my river?'

'They *are* water creatures,' said Nan.

'And it's my water,' grumbled Mr Pernicky, 'so I'm going to get rid of them, no matter what it takes!'

The walls of Mr Pernicky's home were covered with tools and bookshelves full of

building plans. He took a long wooden ruler from the wall, rushed over to a drawer and pulled out a notebook.

'What are you up to now?' asked Nan.

'Making plans,' said Mr Pernicky, and he turned his back on them and sat down to scrawl some notes. 'You should probably leave!'

Grandma Nan shrugged. 'If that's how you want it to be,' she said with frustration.

Rosa and Nan walked back towards the beavers. Even in that short time their lodge had grown bigger and was now standing proud of the water. The building work continued as they watched, with Elsie and Iris chewing and shaping branches to fit their plans.

'This isn't going to end well,' said Nan.

'I've never seen anyone work so hard,' said Rosa.

'They are *definitely* busy,' said Nan.

At that moment a flock of crows flew overhead, squawking and chattering. Rosa heard mentions of the beavers, and of their roosts being lost.

'Looks like Mr Pernicky isn't the only one who isn't happy,' said Rosa.

'Newcomers to the mountain always make a difference, Rosa,' said Nan. 'It just takes time for things to settle, for everyone to find their place.'

'But Mr Pernicky doesn't seem very understanding,' said Rosa. 'Maybe he could try talking to the beavers?'

'He's just struggling with change,' said Nan. 'Sometimes people forget that life never stays still for long. I certainly wasn't expecting you to come and stay with me.'

Rosa fell quiet. Did she not like having her about?

'Anyway,' said Nan, walking on, 'more importantly, the daylight is fading. We won't be making it home tonight.'

Rosa didn't take the news well.

'What about the wolves?' she asked.

'They don't like humans,' said Nan. 'I doubt they'll come anywhere near us – I promise – especially if we keep our fire lit.'

'Are you totally sure?' asked Rosa. 'Absolutely, totally, one hundred per cent certain?'

'Hey, when was the last time you saw the stars?' asked Nan, who was very good at changing subjects when things got tricky to explain.

'Just the other week,' said Rosa. 'Back in the city.'

'No, no, no!' laughed Nan. 'When was the last time you *really* saw the stars out in the open? Where the sky is filled with the glowing star clouds of the Milky Way?'

'Oh. Well, I've never seen that,' admitted Rosa.

Grandma Nan smiled and put her arm round Rosa. 'Then tonight you have a real treat in store,' she said. 'There is nowhere better to see stars than Big Sky Mountain!'

9

Under the Stars

Once they'd found the perfect spot near the river, they set about making camp. With Rosa's help, Nan built a shelter from branches and string, with a thin waterproof sheet stretched tight over its top.

'There we are!' said Nan, slapping the sheet like a drum. It made a pleasing 'doink' noise. 'That'll keep us dry if it rains.'

Rosa hadn't slept outdoors before, but even in the pure darkness of the night-time forest, it felt safe enough.

'Won't we get cold?' she asked.

'Don't you worry about that,' said Nan. 'We'll get a little fire going and all will be well.'

Nan placed down her torch with the beam still on and set to making a fire. Nan was an old hand at the life outdoors, and always carried a little tin full of everything that she needed to start a fire. With a few well-placed twigs and a handful of crisp, dry tinder, Nan only needed a spark to set it going. The first few flames took hold instantly.

'Wow,' said Rosa. 'That was like magic.'

'Oh, it's easy, my girl,' said Nan. 'If you're careful and prepare it all properly, that is. I'll teach you. Don't you worry.'

Rosa felt so excited, and, despite what Nan said, it really was magic. Fire sprites danced up into the sky, skittishly moving through the treetops, and the fire's burning heart shimmered blue then golden yellow like a dragon's flame.

Wrapped up in blankets, Rosa and Nan nestled down to enjoy the evening, feeling safe and warm. Lone songs of night birds and the shouts of grumpy owls coloured the air, and every now and then moths and midges fluttered and buzzed nearby, passing judgement on some matter or other.

And as for the stars, Nan was right.

The sky looked unlike anything Rosa had ever experienced. Huge clusters of shimmering blue and pink stars formed a rippling backbone across the heavens.

'Why don't we have them like this in the city?' asked Rosa.

'Because of the street lights polluting the skies,' said Nan. 'But without the lamps I guess you'd always be tripping over someone or other.'

'Hmm,' agreed Rosa, lying back. The stars filled her with a peculiar sense of calm.

Seeing them made everything feel all right.

'You take the first sleep,' said Nan. 'I'll wake you in a few hours and then you can keep watch, all right?'

All of Rosa's fears slipped away, as the crackling fire and ripples of the river lulled her into a deep sleep. When Nan eventually woke her the fire was still burning – a little lower than before – but there was an odd knocking noise echoing through the forest.

'What's that?' asked Rosa with a yawn.

'Someone's busy building,' said Nan.

'The beavers?' said Rosa. 'Still?'

'I didn't see them with tools,' said Nan wisely. 'No, I think this is Mr Pernicky up to something.'

She crawled back under her blanket and left Rosa to keep watch.

'Just a few hours,' muttered Nan.

'Yes,' said Rosa.

But Rosa found it increasingly hard to stay awake, and before she knew it, her eyes were closing once again.

10

Beaver Battles

Rosa sat bolt upright. The campfire was out and the sky was glowing a rich turquoise blue with the onset of day. The patch of ground around her looked different to the previous night, and it took a few moments for her to register why.

'NAN!' shouted Rosa. 'Wake up!'

The river had swollen overnight, and water was lapping just a few metres from her feet. She was close to getting drenched.

'Whut . . .?' said Nan. She sat up, her hair decorated with pine needles and twigs. She rubbed her eyes.

'The water, Nan!' said Rosa. 'It's almost on us! I fell asleep; I'm so sorry.'

'Oh, don't worry,' said Nan. 'But water? Here?'

She found her glasses and was suddenly able to see what had happened for herself.

'Well, blow my trumpet,' she said, getting to her feet. 'It's them beavers! They don't half work hard.'

'The beavers did this?' said Rosa, quite amazed at what they were capable of. 'Elsie said she had plans, but . . .'

'They definitely work fast!' said Nan. 'I hadn't imagined they'd finish their dams overnight.'

Grandma Nan paused, realising the downside to the beavers' actions.

'We best go and see Mr Pernicky,' she said with a grumble. 'He's not going to like this, is he?'

They hurriedly rolled up their blankets, dismantled their shelter and packed it all away. Mr Pernicky's house was now sitting slap bang in the middle of a pond, with half its door submerged.

'Oh no,' said Rosa.

'Just as I feared,' said Nan.

A huge cry rang out from the cabin.

'WHHAAAAAAAAAAT!?!' screamed Mr Pernicky.

Grandma Nan waded into the pond and tried to open the cabin door.

'It's only me,' she said. 'Let me help you.'

'It's ruined!' he cried. 'They've turned my home into a fish tank!'

The door opened, and a furious Mr Pernicky appeared. His face was berry red in anger.

'I WILL NOT STAND FOR THIS,' he snarled.

He pushed past Nan and hopped off into the forest.

'What's he up to?' asked Rosa.

'Your guess is as good as mine,' said Nan. 'Come on. Let's see what the beavers have to say for themselves.'

The beavers had clearly not stopped working through the night either. Their lodge was now a mound of branches, twigs and mud in the middle of the river.

PLOP!

Elsie was in the process of building a house on its top, weaving together walls of willow saplings and reeds.

'Is that Iris?' called Nan from a distance. The beavers were so alike it was impossible to tell, even close up. Nan had no idea where the river's edge was any more, so she dared not step any closer.

'It's Elsie,' said the beaver.

'Ah, sorry, my eyesight's not what it was,' said Nan.

'Happens all the time!' said Elsie.

'Have you seen what's happened to Mr Pernicky's cabin?' asked Rosa. 'You've flooded his home.'

'Oh my days!' said Elsie. Her tail slapped against the water, and Iris's head popped up from among a cluster of floating branches. 'We've only gone and flooded that hare's house!' said Elsie.

'You're kidding?!' said Iris, climbing out of the water.

'It's up to his waist,' said Rosa.

'Now we'll be even less popular,' said Iris. She scratched her damp fur. 'Is it bad?'

BOING!!

'Very,' said Nan. Suddenly they all heard a loud 'TWANG!' and a volley of mud bombs flew over their heads and splashed into the water.

'I'll show you flea-bitten furballs!' shouted Mr Pernicky.

'He's built a catapult!' said Rosa.

'So that was what all the banging was about,' said Nan.

The hare started rearming the rough and ready weapon for a second round.

'Wait, Mr Pernicky!' shouted Grandma Nan.

Another mud bomb flew past her ear and smashed into the beavers' building site.

'We're under attack,' said Iris.

'I am not putting up with this!'
announced Elsie. She threw down the
branch that was in her paws.

'Now, stop right there, you two!' said
Grandma Nan. 'We can sort this out like
civilised creatures.'

'That hare is anything but civilised,'
said Iris. 'Come on!'

The two beavers slipped into the
river and vanished, as another mud
bomb rocketed out of the woods and
smashed into the beavers' lodge. Nan was

splattered from head to toe with twigs
and dirt.

'Nan!' cried Rosa. 'Get away from
there! Head for cover!'

BLAM!

11

The Splatter Matter

Rosa and Nan huddled beside a tree as
mud bombs splattered left, right and centre.

'We've got to stop him!' said Rosa. 'He
might hurt someone.'

'I'm not sure I know how to stop a
hare in a rage,' said Nan. 'It's normally
best to let him calm down.'

'But he'll destroy everything!' said
Rosa.

There was a twang, and more mud bombs hurtled into the air. Rosa and Nan looked to the skies. The heavy mud balls seemed to hang in the air, then exploded into the tree trunk that protected Rosa and Nan. It shocked them both, and Nan tumbled backwards on to the muddy ground. Despite her determined frown, Rosa thought she looked suddenly fragile.

'Grandma Nan! Are you hurt?' asked Rosa.

'No, I'm absolutely fine,' said Nan defiantly, righting the glasses on her nose.

'It's just that some crazy hare is firing weapons at us!'

Rosa knew Nan was shaken, and trying not to show it.

'You must be more careful,' said Rosa, helping Nan to her feet.

'I'm not some doddery old stick, you know,' said Nan. 'I am always careful!'

'Then be *more* careful,' urged Rosa.

Grandma Nan huffed and tested out her legs.

'No! My ankle's twisted,' she said, wincing as she lowered her foot to the ground.

'Can you walk?' asked Rosa.

'Yes, I can walk,' said Nan.

Another flurry of mud bombs splashed into the river.

'And it's time to put an end to this nonsense,' said Nan. 'Come on.'

But Grandma Nan wasn't fooling anyone. She struggled with every step, and Rosa knew she had to do something. Would Grandma Nan listen to her? she wondered.

'Stop! Stop now!' said Rosa.

'Do not tell me what to do,' said Nan, struggling on.

Rosa had to be bolder. If Grandma Nan hurt herself further, they could be in real trouble getting home. Rosa ran ahead and blocked Nan's path.

'Please, Grandma Nan!' pleaded Rosa.

Grandma Nan looked like thunder about to erupt, and Rosa's confidence evaporated. In the silence of Grandma

Nan's stare the seconds felt like hours. Finally Rosa dug in her heels and plucked up the courage to speak again.

'If you get any worse, how will we walk back to the canoe? How will we get home?'

Grandma Nan was stubborn, but she wasn't stupid. She lifted her glasses and rubbed her eyes.

'Well, that told me,' she said. Her stormy mood had moved on, and she eased herself to the ground with something of a smile. 'Do you think you can stop Mr Pernicky alone?'

'I can try,' said Rosa, and she marched off to speak with the hare. He laughed manically as one of his mud bombs struck the beavers' lodge. His arms were filled

with three more large balls of mud, ready
to fire.

'I've almost blasted a hole through it!'
he cried.

'This has to end, Mr Pernicky!' said
Rosa. 'Now!'

Rosa was feeling more confident
than ever after persuading her grandma
to rest. Mr Pernicky, however, was a
very different kettle of fish. He was
definitely not one to back down,
especially when he was enjoying himself
so much.

'Absolutely not,' he said. 'Haven't had
so much fun in years.'

He pulled back the catapult, and
loaded up the bombs.

'But you could hurt someone!' said

Rosa. 'There are better ways of sorting things out!'

'I don't believe there are,' he said curtly.

Rosa heard a peculiar creaking squeal, and the beavers shouted 'TIMBER!' at the top of their voices.

Mr Pernicky's eyes grew unbelievably wide. His ears shot upright.

'Get out of the way!' cried Rosa.

She gripped him in her hands and pushed him to one side as a huge tree – gnawed fully in two by the beavers – came careering down right on top of his

catapult. The trunk smashed it to splinters without so much as an argument.

Mr Pernicky's ears flopped to his side in defeat.

'THAT'S ENOUGH!' ordered Rosa. 'Grandma Nan is hurt, and it's a wonder all of us are still in one piece.'

CRASH!

The beavers shuffled out from behind the gnawed tree trunk. Rosa's shouting had left them feeling mighty sheepish.

'Nan's hurt?' asked Mr Pernicky.

'Yes,' said Rosa. 'You should all be ashamed.'

'But they flooded my house and ruined my carrots!' said Mr Pernicky.

'We didn't think we were causing any harm,' said Elsie. 'We were just building *our* new home.'

Mr Pernicky muttered something mean.

Rosa was determined to solve the matter. 'I don't think they meant to do this,' she said.

'They knew exactly what they were doing,' said Mr Pernicky. 'Those beavers are masters of chopping things up and flooding everything. Besides, they are intruders on my land. I've lived here forever without anyone and I am perfectly happy.'

'We are not intruders,' said Iris. 'We were told we could move here. And we do no harm.'

'You must admit, you have changed the forest,' said Rosa.

Elsie blushed. 'I suppose we have chopped down a *few* trees,' she said.

'And everyone needs to be thoughtful of others' feelings,' said Rosa, carefully.

'My feelings are that they should go away,' said Mr Pernicky.

There was a loud whooshing noise, as the river eventually broke through the beavers' damaged dam. The water surrounding the hare's home started to disperse.

Mr Pernicky was overjoyed. Elsie and Iris were devastated.

'I'm sorry about that,' said Rosa. 'You'd worked so hard on it.'

'Beaver Town was going to be

awesome,' said Iris.

'And now all is back to normal,' said Mr Pernicky happily. He clapped his paws and made to hop off home.

'No,' said Rosa, firmly blocking his path. 'These beavers are now part of the mountain. You need to find a way to live together and work together.'

'Why?' said Mr Pernicky.

Rosa tried to remember all the things her grandma had said. She knew it was important to say the correct words.

'Because we all have a right to be here,' she said. 'Who gave you the right to build your home?'

Mr Pernicky was silent.

'Who told you this was your river?' added Rosa.

Mr Pernicky again had no answer.

'With a little effort everyone can live together happily,' said Rosa. 'We all have a role to play in looking after the mountain.'

Mr Pernicky's ears flopped down. 'All right,' he grumbled.

Elsie and Iris were glowing with happiness.

'Now sit down here and find a way to get along,' said Rosa. 'You can all get along, I know it.'

A Helping Hand

Rosa returned to her grandma, who hadn't moved, but had made a daisy chain the length of her arm.

'Not a single mud bomb for at least ten minutes!' said Grandma Nan. 'You must have done well, Rosa.'

'I think the beavers were better at stopping Mr Pernicky than me,' she replied. 'How's your ankle?'

Grandma Nan pulled down her sock. Her foot was as swollen and wide as an ancient oak tree, and it had turned a gruesome shade of purple.

'Ouch! Ouch! Ouch!' Rosa said. 'It looks bad.'

Grandma Nan agreed. 'It's a good job you told me to rest,' she said. She patted Rosa on the leg with thanks. It wasn't easy for Grandma Nan to admit that Rosa had been correct, but she always believed in being honest. 'It filled up like a balloon as soon as I sat down.'

Rosa looked a little bit squeamish at the thought. 'Can you walk at all?' she asked.

'Only one way to find out,' said Nan. But Grandma Nan screwed up her

face in pain as she
tried to stand,
and Rosa knew
their problems
had only just
begun.

'How will
we get you
back up
Dilly-dally Falls?' she asked.

'I'll manage,' said Nan. But not even
she believed herself.

Nan hobbled slowly to the waterfall,
bag on her back, half slumped over
Rosa's shoulder. One look up the narrow
track along its edge told her she could go
no further.

'Pains me to say it,' said Nan, staring

up at the roaring waterfall. 'But I think we'll need Tom to tie me to his aeroplane to get me up there.'

Rosa let Nan down gently and gazed thoughtfully at the track. There was no easy way round it.

'We're stuck,' she said.

They both scratched their heads in thought.

'I suppose we could rest here another night,' said Nan. 'See if my ankle gets better. We have a little more food, and your honey.'

Rosa considered setting up camp again when two shadows emerged from the depths of the river. The beavers broke out of the water, and pulled themselves up the riverbank.

'Elsie! Iris!' said Rosa.

'We were too busy worrying about ourselves to take in that Nan had been hurt,' said Iris. 'We're sorry.'

'It's nothing,' said Nan.

'Your ankle is not nothing,' said Rosa. 'We can't get home. She can't walk up there.'

Rosa pointed to the top of the waterfall.

'That is a problem,' said Iris, measuring the distance with her paws and eyes. 'But I think we can help. Yes?'

Elsie nodded furiously. 'YES WE CAN!' she cried, proudly slamming her paws into her hips. 'We are builders! We can find a way.'

Elsie's enthusiasm vanished instantly.

'We'll need Mr Pernicky's help,' she added.

'Don't put yourselves out on my part,' said Nan.

The beavers were having none of it.

'Don't move,' said Iris.

'No fear of that,' said Nan.

The beavers returned a short while later, tugging a flotilla of chewed fallen

logs upstream. Mr Pernicky was balanced precariously on top, a long rope wrapped round his shoulder, tool in one paw and some paper plans in the other. His ears were bolt upright, and he looked like he meant business.

'Sit tight, Nan!' he ordered, hopping from the logs on to the riverbank. 'We'll have you up there in a jiffy!'

Rosa watched with fascination as the hare and the beavers conversed over the plans, nodding and agreeing with great conviction. With smiles and determination all round they set to work.

Elsie scampered up the narrow path to the top, leant over the edge and threw down two ropes to Iris below. They secured them in place, while Mr Pernicky chopped and hammered branches and lumps of timber, following his design.

Before long he'd knocked up a structure solid enough to take Nan's weight. With a little bit of invention Mr Pernicky joined the ropes and a broken old seat from his home, and secured it to the ground.

'What do you think of that then?' said Mr Pernicky proudly. 'Pull it up, Elsie!'

The beaver tugged at one of the ropes, and the rickety seat lifted easily into the air, climbing towards the top of the waterfall.

'It works!' said Iris.

'What did you think it would do?!' snapped Mr Pernicky.

'Ingenious!' said Grandma Nan. 'They've built a winch.'

'Hop on then!' said Mr Pernicky.

'Are you feeling brave enough?' asked Rosa to Grandma Nan.

'What choice do I have?' she replied, smiling bravely.

Mr Pernicky dragged the seat back to the ground and jumped in. He bounced up and down to prove its strength.

'See!' he said. 'Hare ingenuity! Never lets you down.'

With Rosa's assistance Nan took the hare's place. She gripped the seat tightly.

'Ready?' said Iris.

'See you at the top,' said Nan. 'Thank you, Mr Pernicky!'

'Hold on!' he said, and with a swift tug of the ropes Nan was hoisted up and over the roaring waterfall. She cackled with laughter at the wide-ranging view from its top. Big Sky Mountain had never seemed so exciting as when hanging in the air.

'I'm flying!' cried Grandma Nan joyfully.

Rosa hurried up the path to meet her grandma at the top of the waterfall. She helped her out of the seat, and pulled the canoe down into the river ready for boarding.

'We made it!' said Rosa.

'Yes we did, my love!' said Grandma Nan.

Rosa smiled happily. She gave her grandma a huge hug, taking Nan by surprise — eventually Nan thought to put her arms round her granddaughter and squeeze back.

'You must come and visit us again,' said Elsie. 'We'll soon have Beaver Town up and running.'

'I would like that a lot!' said Rosa.

Then they waved goodbye to Iris and Mr Pernicky, and settled into *Florence* with their bags. With the oar in her hands, Rosa pulled off into the river and steered them home.

13

Home Again

Little Pig greeted Rosa and Nan at the shoreline, and informed them there had been no intruders, or wolves, or anything else in any way scary.

'I am still alive!' he said.

But he quickly noticed Nan's ankle.
'Unlike you!?' he added, shrieking
upwards into the sky. 'What have you
done? What have you done?'

Nan hobbled up the shore to her cabin,
aided by Rosa.

'It's just a sprain,' she said calmly. 'I
simply need to put my feet up for the next
few days.'

'I'll look after her,' said Rosa.

'I'll have to keep an even better watch!'
said Little Pig, fretting. 'Yes! That's exactly
what I'll do.'

He slid into his resting place under
the roof and opened his eyes wide. Rosa
laughed and opened the cabin door.
She dropped the bag to the ground and
helped Nan on to her bed.

'I'm very pleased you've come to stay with me, Rosa,' said Nan. 'I know I might not have been so welcoming when you arrived, but I can see you are a Wild through and through.'

These words filled Rosa with joy. She sat on the edge of the bed, feeling contented and not a little exhausted.

She started to daydream about life on the mountain – there was so much of it she had yet to see.

'I suppose we should get some food on the go,' said Nan, who struggled to stay still for any length of time. 'Fancy a pot of beans?'

Rosa was starving, and she knew everything took much longer to do on the mountain than it used to in the city. Cooking any meal now took hours, and she knew she would have to do all the work.

'I'll get it going,' she said, easing herself up.

'There are herbs outside in the veg patch,' said Nan. 'And packs of dried beans in the cupboard. Also, onions in the –'

'Don't worry, I'll find it all,' said Rosa.

She was beginning to see that Grandma Nan was going to make the worst patient ever.

As Rosa opened a cupboard there was a bump and a rattle outside the cabin.

'What's this?' said Albert the Moose, his head lurching through the open window. 'Hooman calf still here?'

'That's right, Albert,' said Nan.

'She don't smell quite so much of pretty flowers no more,' said Albert.

'No, she doesn't,' said Nan. 'Apple?'

Albert started to slobber. 'Yes, please!' he said.

Rosa tossed an apple to him and he caught it in his mouth. With much effort he tried to remove his head and huge antlers from the window, but after three attempts he gave up.

'Stupid head,' he said. 'I'll eat it here.'

'Good idea,' said Nan.

'Good idea,' said Rosa.

14

The Story

A few days later, when the weather was fine and Grandma Nan's ankle was nearly back to its normal size, Mr Hibberdee arrived at the lake. Rosa had been chopping some wood under the watchful gaze of Albert the Moose, and she spotted the bear trundling through the scrub without a care in the world. Rosa waved happily.

'Good morning,' said Mr Hibberdee, his scarf fluttering in the breeze.

'Hello,' said Rosa, wiping her brow. 'How are you and your jams?'

'Sweet as ever,' he said thoughtfully. 'I wondered if you might have payment for my honey?'

Rosa's heart started to race – she had pushed the matter right out of her mind.

'Well,' she said tentatively, 'Grandma Nan mentioned that you might like a story in payment?'

Mr Hibberdee's face brightened.

'Oh, yes!' he said, scratching his neck. 'I haven't heard a story in weeks. But make sure it's exciting. I love exciting stories.'

'I can try?' said Rosa.

Mr Hibberdee clapped with happiness,

and sat down on a fallen tree trunk at the lakeside. They watched a flock of geese bob up and down on the water as Rosa started to tell her story. She took a deep breath.

'When Dad couldn't look after me any more in the city, Grandma Nan was the only person I could think of who might put me up. I'd never met her before, but I had to try,' she said.

Sad stories always affected Mr Hibberdee the most. His eyes sparkled. 'And?'

'So I wrote her a letter,' laughed Rosa. 'But Grandma Nan can't remember that bit.'

Mr Hibberdee let out a rumbly sort of laugh.

'And then Tom flew me here in his little plane,' said Rosa.

'You flew here in an aeroplane?' said Mr Hibberdee excitedly.

'Yes. A little one,' said Rosa. 'And it could land on water!'

'Wow,' said Mr Hibberdee. 'I should love to travel in an aeroplane one day. It would make getting to my customers easier, that's for sure. Bears don't often get the chance to fly.'

'No, I bet they don't,' said Rosa.

'I doubt we'd fit in the seats,' said Mr Hibberdee. 'And I hear they only serve tiny packets of jam. That would be no good.'

'You'd have to take your own,' said Rosa.

'I would!' said Mr Hibberdee. 'And do you like it here?'

Rosa paused to think. She'd only spent a few days on Big Sky Mountain, but she'd already seen and done so much.

'I think I do,' said Rosa. 'It really is like no other place on Earth. I've sailed in a canoe. I slept under a waterfall. I met some busy beavers, and a really angry hare – although he seemed all right in the end. And I also saw all the stars in the galaxy.'

'*All* the stars?' said the bear excitedly.

'Yes, I think so,' said Rosa.

'Wow,' said Mr Hibberdee. 'What a story!' He growled and dug around in his backpack for another jar of honey. 'Would you like some more?'

'I still don't have any money,' said Rosa.

'Your stories are worth more than money to me, Rosa,' he said. He lifted a big furry eyebrow, and Rosa agreed. She took the jar. 'It's a pleasure doing business with you,' he said.

And with that Mr Hibberdee picked up his things and strolled off along the lake.

'Everything good?' called Grandma Nan from the cabin.

Rosa gathered the firewood and crunched her way back up the shore with the new jar of honey.

'Yes, it is,' said Rosa. 'Everything is perfect.'

Can you find?

Can you help Rosa find these hidden
species on Big Sky Mountain?
They're all somewhere in the book.

Yellow Iris

Hazel

Bulrushes

Red Campion

Place a tick under each box as you find them!

(Answers at the bottom of the page.)

Wood Anenome

Silver Birch Catkins

Cep Mushrooms

Foxgloves

Cabins

I really love cabins.

Cabins can be found anywhere, but they're mostly found in the middle of nowhere, and that's what makes them so special. Because they're often so far from towns and shops, they're usually very simple designs, made from logs or boards of wood. Some might even be made of stone.

I think this is what I like the most about cabins: they've all been built by hand and no two look the same. They might have a roof covered with earth and grass, they might be built out of an upturned boat, or they might even be made from a huge old wooden barrel.

But why do people stay in cabins? Well, they're sometimes a home, or a place to go on holiday, but they can also be places for times of need. Some cabins are stocked with food and firewood, for mountain wanderers needing a place to spend the night.

I made Grandma Nan's cabin really simple, as she didn't need anything too grand to live in. But I wonder if you were to build your own cabin, how would it look? Would it be on a mountain, or next to a lake? Or maybe in a huge forest?

Perhaps you could try drawing your own!

A Note from Alex

Big Sky Mountain is based on my childhood adventures with my grandma. But it's also about the wilderness, and living free in a landscape full of animals big and small.

My unflappable gran was a force of nature. She would be the first into the sea, even if it was a freezing day. She lived in a town called Malvern, which is most famous for its beautiful hills and the composer Edward Elgar. Whenever we visited, Gran would march us up the hills whatever the weather. There was always an adventure to be had, and we'd always return home safe, if exhausted –

My brother Robin, Gran and me up the hills.

while Gran had energy to spare.

Rosa is very much like me. I love getting up mountains and walking along rivers, so I had a lot of fun showing Rosa experiencing the wilderness for the first time, tasting the magic of a magnificent starlit night, and feeling the rush and roar of paddling a canoe down a river. And most of all, I loved showing her learning to care for all the new friends she meets on Big Sky Mountain, while respecting them and their very different ways.

Once upon a time, Britain was filled with now-extinct animals like aurochs, woolly rhinos and mammoths, and more recently wolves and badgers. Just by going about their daily business, these animals helped to keep the landscape healthy and alive. By knocking down trees, digging up

the soil, slowing down rivers, they helped
create fertile breeding grounds for young
creatures or seeds and saplings – all
without any help from humans!

We can help our remaining wildernesses
by bringing back some of these creatures
to our landscape, but nature is also good at
looking after itself, if allowed.

I truly feel that every creature on this
planet is connected, in one way or another.
The tiniest insect is just as important as the
bawdiest elephant and ultimately every
human. Just like Grandma Nan and Rosa,
I always try to leave no trace and do no
harm to others, because I believe we can
and should live peacefully alongside the
animals of this world.

I certainly want to, don't you?